She's Wearing a Dead Bird on Her Head!

Kathryn Lasky   Illustrated by David Catrow

Hyperion Paperbacks for Children
New York

For Anne Warren Weld (1912–1992),
who never wore a dead bird on her head and
carried on where Harriet and Minna left off
—K.L.

To Mom and Dad, who sometimes let me fly
—D.C.

First Hyperion Paperback edition 1997

Text © 1995 by Kathryn Lasky.
Illustrations © 1995 by David Catrow.

Printed in Singapore.

3 5 7 9 10 8 6 4 2

Library of Congress Cataloging-in-Publication Data
Lasky, Kathryn.
She's wearing a dead bird on her head / Kathryn Lasky;
illustrated by David Catrow—1st ed.
p.   cm.
Summary: A fictionalized account of the activities of Harriet Hemenway and Minna Hall, founders of the Massachusetts Audubon Society, a late nineteenth-century Audubon Society that would endure and have impact on the bird-protection movement.
ISBN 0-7868-0065-8 (trade)—ISBN 0-7868-2052-7 (lib. bdg.)—ISBN 0-7868-1164-1 (pbk.)
[1. Hemenway, Harriet—Fiction. 2. Hall, Minna—Fiction.
3. Massachusetts Audubon Society—Fiction. 4. Birds—Protection—
Fiction.] I. Catrow, David, ill. II. Title.
PZ8.3.L335Sh   1995   [Fic]—dc20   94-18204

The artwork for each picture was prepared using watercolor and ink.

She's Wearing a Dead Bird on Her Head!

Harriet Hemenway was a very proper Boston lady—she never talked with her mouth full. But one day she almost did. Standing by the bay window in her parlor, she had just bitten into a jam cookie when her eyes sprang open in dismay. She gasped, leaned forward, swallowed, then turned to her parlor maid.

"She's wearing a dead bird on her head!"

Feathers on ladies' hats were becoming more and more popular. At first, hats had been decorated with just feathers, and then designers began to add pairs of wings. But this woman had an entire bird perched atop her hat! Harriet squinted her eyes as the lady of fashion walked proudly by. "Arctic tern, I believe," Harriet whispered.

"Looks ready to fly away," said the parlor maid.

"It won't," Harriet replied sadly.

Harriet felt that she had to do something. Huge populations of birds, from egrets to pheasants to owls to warblers, were being slaughtered for hat decoration—none were spared. Not even pigeons! But what could she do? Women in 1896 had very little power. They could not vote, and many had husbands who did not allow them to make decisions for themselves. Some women were not even allowed to read newspapers! Harriet's husband, Augustus, did not treat her this way.

But she and other women like her wanted to change things for *all* women. And she wanted to do something for the birds. Fashion was killing birds as well as killing women's chances to have the right to vote and be listened to. For who would listen to a woman with a dead bird on her head? And if the senseless slaughter for a silly fashion was not stopped, in a few years the birds with the prettiest feathers would all be dead, gone forever, extinct.

"I must call cousin Minna," Harriet said grimly.

Click, click, click, click. The heels of Miss Minna Hall's high-buttoned shoes beat a quick rhythm against the bricks of the sidewalk. Her blue eyes were bright as they searched the bare limbs of the trees that lined the avenue for the yellow finches that appeared like spots of flitting gold on this gray winter day. Their quick golden flight swelled her heart.

Click, click, click, click. She could not be late for tea at Harriet's. This was too important. *Click, click, click, click.* Miss Hall's feet froze in their tracks. Straight ahead there was indeed a pair of golden wings, but they had neither head nor body attached. They were pinned instead to the crown of a lady's hat, and on the brim was a swirl of snowy egret feathers.

"Revolting!" The single word rumbled down Commonwealth Avenue as noisily as a cannonball loose on a ship's deck.

"Me!" the fashionable lady squeaked with dismay.

"You, you heartless creature! That a bird should be slaughtered just to make you feel pretty. Yecccch!" Minna made a scalding sound deep in the back of her throat.

When Minna stormed into the parlor, Harriet was preparing tea.

"Well, Harriet," Minna exclaimed as she pulled off her felt cap. "From Arlington Street to Clarendon—three egrets, one marabou, two grebes, one golden finch, and . . ." Minna paused. Her cousin waited nervously, the teacup chattering on the saucer she was holding. "A hummingbird!"

"Oh no, Minna!"

"Oh yes, Harriet—perched in full flight on a bunch of silk roses with a veil."

"Disgusting!"

"Revolting!"

"Nauseating!"

"Vile!"

The words flew through the air like red-hot cinders.

"Well, let's get down to business," Minna said. "Do you have the book?"

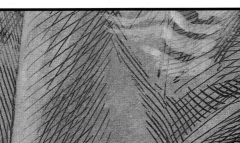

"Yes, right here." Harriet Hemenway walked over to a shelf in the parlor and took down a large blue volume. The words *Boston Social Register* were written across the cover in gold letters. The book was a list of all the grandest families in Boston.

They opened the book, and with pencils in hand they began to scan the list of families, starting with A.

"Mrs. Appleton, quite fashionable."

"Indeed! A peafowl with a few warbler feathers at tea last week."

"Bancroft?"

"Marabou fan and hat to match at the opera."

Finally, they got to Z.

"Mrs. Zacharias?"

"Egrets and warblers, with a touch of flamingo, I do believe, luncheon at the Somerset Hotel."

"Dear, dear . . ." Minna moaned and sipped the last of her tea. "What shall we do?"

"Well." Harriet scratched her head. "We have garden clubs and history clubs—why not form a bird club! Not to just watch birds, no, but to protect them and stop this senseless murdering for fashion."

"What a wonderful idea," said Minna. "Let's do it. Let's start a club for the birds."

Right then they began to write letters to all the Boston ladies of fashion who wore the plumage of birds, imploring them to put aside their fancy hats with swirls of owl feathers, breasts of grebes, wings of hummingbirds, and plumes of egrets and instead join a society dedicated to protecting all birds. This was the first informal meeting of the Audubon Society, named after a man they admired, John Audubon, the famous painter of birds.

Harriet and Minna were very persuasive. They convinced women not only that killing birds was wrong but that birds as hat decoration made women look silly. Soon many of the fashionable ladies of Boston to whom they had written letters did join the society.

For the club to accomplish its goals, however, Harriet and Minna knew it also needed men—smart, powerful men who could vote and go into public places like the state legislatures and the halls of Congress in Washington, D.C. So they asked lawyers and doctors, sportsmen, and bird experts to join, too.

At the second meeting of the Audubon Society, Harriet and Minna and the new members made up rules for their club.

"I think," said one gentleman, "that there should be an exception made for ducks."

"What kind of exception?" Harriet asked.

"We want to hunt them," replied another gentleman.

"Rules are rules," fumed Minna.

"Sportsmen aren't special," another woman said, and stamped her foot.

The women won. There would be no killing of ducks or game birds. Then all the members devised a plan to get the word out on birds to everyone. And the Bird Hat Campaign of the Audubon Society began in earnest.

They decided to bring their cause to the children of the state of Massachusetts. So into the schools they went—Minna, Harriet, and other members of the society.

"In Florida, heaps of birds, stripped of their feathers, are left dying on the ground," Harriet told one class of children, holding up a photograph of a pile of dead egrets.

"What happened to their babies, the ones left in the nest?" a student asked.

"The ones that are too young to fly are left to die. So you see, we need your help, the *birds* need your help, to protect them against the plume hunters and the hatmakers. Please join our club."

Soon there were over ten thousand junior members of the Audubon Society in the state of Massachusetts. And Audubon societies were formed in other states. More children joined.

The membership in Boston continued to grow, and the meetings were always lively.

"The orange groves in Florida this year are suffering because there are too many dead hummingbirds on hats and not enough in the groves eating the pests that spoil the fruit," said Miss Harriet Richards, the secretary of the society.

"Let's get the farmers on our side. Send out a letter!" Minna said.

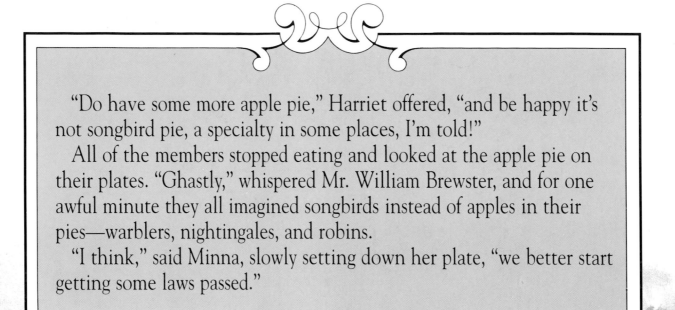

"Do have some more apple pie," Harriet offered, "and be happy it's not songbird pie, a specialty in some places, I'm told!"

All of the members stopped eating and looked at the apple pie on their plates. "Ghastly," whispered Mr. William Brewster, and for one awful minute they all imagined songbirds instead of apples in their pies—warblers, nightingales, and robins.

"I think," said Minna, slowly setting down her plate, "we better start getting some laws passed."

In the club everybody was equal. The women and the men of the society wrote up their ideas together and then sent the gentlemen to talk to legislators in the State House and to members of Congress in Washington, D.C., to press for the passage of laws to save the birds. They were successful! An act was passed in 1903 to protect herons and bitterns, two popular hat birds, from hatmakers, forbidding them to sell, display, or possess the feathers. In 1904 there was another victory when a law was passed to protect shore, marsh, and beach birds.

HEATH HEN

DODO

Soon there were laws against hunting birds during their breeding seasons. And then a federal law was passed preventing the importation of feathers from Europe and the tropics for hats. The word about birds had spread all the way to England, where Queen Victoria had announced that she would never again wear a feather for fashion.

But Minna and Harriet were still far from happy.

"What good is a law if it isn't enforced," Minna moaned one day as she stood looking out the window at a woman passing by with a pheasant's wing raking the air above her. "You can't arrest the lady for wearing the hat."

"But you can arrest the supplier of the feather," Harriet said. She tapped her head lightly as if to give a little jostle to her brains. "There are rumors about secret feather warehouses." She spoke softly. "I think we should make a few inquiries."

So the two ladies, with Harriet's husband, Augustus, took the train to New York City, where they were not so well known. They got as gussied up as two Boston ladies who loved birds and hated fashion could manage. They sashayed down Fifth Avenue in fancy dresses and wore elaborate hats with streamers and ribbons—but no feathers! Into the fanciest hat store the two cousins and Augustus Hemenway pranced.

"I want to buy my wife and dear cousin each a hat, a feathered hat," Augustus announced.

The salespeople began fluttering around the prosperous-looking threesome.

"What will it be, madams? Egrets or doves? A dear little cloche covered with owl feathers or this broad-brimmed hat with the arctic tern? Is it not spectacular on the blue felt, just as if it is plunging into the sea?"

The two ladies swallowed their disgust and muffled their anger. After all, there were more important things at stake.

By the end of the shopping expedition they, alas, had to buy two hats, but they also had the name of the feather supplier with a warehouse in Baltimore where millions of dead birds and tons of plumes were stored. With this information they went directly to the authorities.

Baltimore

Soon after, on a rainy May day, the cousins sat sipping tea. Harriet had just bitten into a crisp wafer when like a tidal wave Augustus burst into the parlor.

"Ladies!" He held a newspaper aloft in his hand. "You've won!"

"We what?" said Minna. She and Harriet held their breath.

"Won, dear cousin and dear wife! Twenty-six thousand illegal gull skins destined for hats of fashion were seized last night from the Baltimore warehouse. They have shut it down, taken the skins, and arrested the owner." Augustus paused. His rain-slicked face beamed with pride. "The law has been enforced!"

Minna looked at her cousin. "Harriet, we won!"
But Harriet said nothing—for Harriet Hemenway never spoke with her mouth full, even when she won.

Author's Note

Harriet Hemenway (1858–1960) and Minna Hall (1859–1951) were real people. All of the other people mentioned by name in this story were also real and members of the Audubon Society. Much of the information on early activities pursued by the society was gathered by reviewing archival material at the Audubon headquarters in Lincoln, Massachusetts.

At the turn of the twentieth century there were many women like Harriet and Minna who wanted to participate more widely in society. In particular, they wanted the right to vote. Such women were smart enough to realize that, if they wished to be taken seriously, having a dead bird perched on their hat would not further their cause. The bird-hat protest movement became linked in subtle ways with suffrage, the right of voting. I based elements of my story on ideas presented by Jennifer Price's *When Women Were Women, Men Were Men, and Birds Were Hats,* which eloquently describes the links between the two movements in this country.

It should be noted that there is no confirmed record of Harriet and Minna ever going into a hat store to buy hats to determine the source of the illegal plume trade. There were stories, however, of their finding out about an illegal warehouse. I took the liberty of imagining how they might have come upon such information. It did not seem plausible to me, given the social conventions of the times, that these two well-born, gentle, but determined women would set out alone to track down the culprits. A more reasonable course of action, I felt, was one in which they might visit a hat store in the company of Harriet's husband and ask some leading questions. All other incidents in the book are based on true events.

Harriet and Minna were not the first people to become involved in bird protection, and the Massachusetts Audubon Society was not the first Audubon Society. It was, however, the first that endured and had impact. It is generally recognized that the Massachusetts organization started by Harriet and Minna was the driving force behind the bird-protection movement, and the most effective in terms of its impact on legislation and education, and of heightening the awareness of the general public to environmental concerns. The society still exists, and aside from working in a broad range of areas concerning the environment, it has most recently been responsible for reintroducing endangered and threatened populations, including such species as the peregrine falcon, the bald eagle, the loon, and the osprey.

—K.L.